white fur flying

Patricia MacLachlan

white fur flying

MARGARET K. MCELDERRY BOOKS
New York   London   Toronto   Sydney   New Delhi

MARGARET K. McELDERRY BOOKS
An imprint of Simon & Schuster Children's Publishing Division
1230 Avenue of the Americas, New York, New York 10020
This book is a work of fiction. Any references to historical events, real people, or real places are used fictitiously. Other names, characters, places, and events are products of the author's imagination, and any resemblance to actual events or places or persons, living or dead, is entirely coincidental.

MARGARET K. McELDERRY BOOKS is a trademark of Simon & Schuster, Inc.
For information about special discounts for bulk purchases, please contact Simon & Schuster Special Sales at 1-866-506-1949 or business@simonandschuster.com.
The Simon & Schuster Speakers Bureau can bring authors to your live event. For more information or to book an event, contact the Simon & Schuster Speakers Bureau at 1-866-248-3049 or visit our website at www.simonspeakers.com.
Also available in a Margaret K. McElderry Books hardcover edition
Book design by Debra Sfetsios-Conover
The text for this book is set in Baskerville MT.
Manufactured in the United States of America
0715 OFF
First Margaret K. McElderry Books paperback edition April 2014
10 9 8
Library of Congress Cataloging-in-Publication Data
MacLachlan, Patricia.
White fur flying / Patricia MacLachlan.—1st ed.
p. cm.
Summary: A sad and silent nine-year-old boy finds his voice when he moves next to a family that rescues dogs.
ISBN 978-1-4424-2171-4 (hardcover)
[1. Rescue dogs—Fiction. 2. Dogs—Fiction. 3. Human-animal relationships—Fiction. 4. Family problems—Fiction.] I. Title.
PZ7.M2225Whi 2013
[Fic]—dc23
2011046125
ISBN 978-1-4424-2172-1 (pbk)
ISBN 978-1-4424-2173-8 (eBook)

For Sue Carlin and all those who rescue dogs—

And for those who adopt and foster them.

It is a heroic, never-ending job.

And for Kodi.

My thanks to Emily Charest

chapter 1

"Once upon a time there was a wicked queen," said my younger sister, Alice.

She peered out the window at the house over the field and across the small brook. I looked and saw a woman, her hair piled on top of her head, walking up the sidewalk. She was followed by movers carrying furniture.

"The wicked queen had two children. They were bad children and she often punished them."

"Alice!" said Mama from the screened side porch. "Can't you tell a pleasant story?"

Alice was the storyteller in the family, some of her stories filled with hilariously mean characters.

"How did she punish them?" I asked.

"Zoe! Don't encourage her."

I watched my mother through the open door to the porch. She brushed Kodi. She always brushed dogs on the screened porch, then swept all the hair up.

"If I brush them outside," she had said, "the hair blows around and hangs on the trees and bushes."

Kodi was a Great Pyrenees, 140 pounds of white fur. May, almost as big, stood waiting for her turn. There was fur everywhere—porch floor, furniture, and on Mama's jeans. Soon May would be adopted into a new family, and there would be other new dogs, one after the other.

Mama rescued Pyrs, as she called them, and found homes for them so they wouldn't be put to sleep. Once, we had five of them in our house. When they lay on the wood living-room floor, they made a huge, deep white rug.

I watched the movers carry a sapphire

blue velvet couch into the house along with two matching chairs.

Mama came to look out the window too.

"No Great Pyrs on that furniture," I said.

"That's for sure," Mama said. "Not on that beautiful couch and those chairs. There's probably no dogs there at all," said Mama. "Or cats."

"And no children," I said.

We watched a series of tables with carved legs be carried in. And then velvet drapes were carefully lifted by two men.

"She punished her children in the drapes," announced Alice, making me jump. I'd almost forgotten she was there.

"She rolled them up like burritos, so only their heads showed. They couldn't get into trouble that way."

Mama couldn't help laughing.

"You have a way, Alice," she said.

We watched the second pair of bright velvet drapes be carried in.

"I suppose I should be neighborly and invite her over for tea," said Mama.

"Not in this house, Mama," I said. "Not during shedding season."

We watched white fur flying into the room, carried by the summer breezes coming off the porch. Some stuck to Mama's shirt. A clump floated by my nose, so close I caught the satisfying smell of dog.

"You can invite her," said Alice. "She

won't punish you. We don't have drapes."

Mama put one arm around Alice and one around me.

"No. No drapes," she said. "Just dogs."

We watched a wooden carved porch swing being hooked up on the porch.

"We *could* weave drapes from the fur of the dogs," Alice said. "It would make life much more exciting."

Before Mama could answer, a long black car pulled up and a man stepped out.

"And suddenly the king arrives," said Alice in what Daddy called her hushed-wildlife-documentary voice. Usually that voice whispered, "And then the leopard sees its prey."

Even though it was summer, the man

wore a jacket and tie. He opened the passenger door. After a moment a small boy climbed out.

"And the prince!" said Alice, surprised.

The man turned and began to walk up to the house. The boy stood still. Then he turned and stared at our house. He saw us all in the window: a mother, two children, and two huge white dogs. Beside me Kodi's tail began to wag. The boy stared.

Then the man/king turned and came back, taking the boy's hand, pulling him up the sidewalk. The boy kept staring at us until he went up the porch steps and into the house.

"Not a prince," said Alice. "A prisoner."

chapter 2

My father came home just before dinner. He still wore his white vet medical jacket. He carried a large covered cage.

Kodi and May ran up to him, sniffing.

"So, what is this?" asked Mama.

"I saved the life of an African grey parrot today," said Daddy.

"And did the parrot thank you?" asked Mama.

Daddy took the cover off the parrot cage.

"Did you thank me?" said Daddy to the parrot.

"You cahn't know!" said the parrot loudly in a British accent.

My mother laughed.

"She belongs to a woman going into a nursing home. She can't keep him," said my father.

"Feisty woman, I'd say," said Mama.

"What's your name?" asked Alice.

"You cahn't know!" said the parrot.

"Lena," said Daddy. "Lena is her name."

"Lena," repeated Lena.

Kodi and May sidled up closer to the parrot.

"Easy, May," said Mama. "Sometimes these dogs don't like birds."

"Easy, May," said Lena.

Kodi sat and stared.

"Most birds don't talk, do they, Kodi?" said Daddy, scratching Kodi's ears.

"I have a question," said Mama. "What is Lena doing here?"

Daddy grinned. "This question from you," he said. "The dog woman. The rescue angel."

"You got me into it, John," said Mama. "Remember? 'The dogs need saving, Claire.'"

"Lena needs saving too," said Daddy.

"Someone has to keep Lena until we find her a home."

"What do you eat?" I asked Lena.

"You cahn't know!" we all said at the same time. Even Lena. This made Lena laugh. It was a high-pitched, wild sound that made us all laugh. The more we laughed, the more Lena did, and the more we did.

And on and on.

The next day, early, there was morning mist, with sun shining through. I let Kodi and May out into the large fenced-in yard. They ran to the side fence, and I could see the boy from next door standing there. Behind him, the man got into his black car and drove off without a wave.

The boy put out his hand and Kodi nosed it through the fence. The boy smiled, then he looked up and saw me, and his smile went away.

"That's all right," I called, walking down through the wet grass in my bare feet. "That's Kodi. His real name is Kodiak. And May, who's licking your hand. I'm Zoe. What's your name?"

The boy was silent but still stood staring at the dogs. Kodi's tail wagged and the boy smiled again.

"Phillip! Phillip, come away from those beasts!"

The woman with the piled-up hair stood on her porch.

"It's all right," I said to her. "They're good dogs."

"They could bite!" she said loudly, coming down the steps.

She walked across the grass, carefully stepping over the small brook that ran between our houses.

"No, they'd never bite," I said.

"Never," said Mama, suddenly standing behind me. "Not when someone is kind to them. Phillip? Is that your name?" she asked.

He nodded.

"He doesn't speak," said the woman impatiently. "At least not to us. My husband's niece left him with us, and we're keeping him while . . ." She hesitated. "While his parents solve a problem."

"Well, Phillip, you can visit the dogs

anytime," said Mama. "You don't have to talk."

Phillip looked at my mother for a long time.

"And you are welcome to visit too," Mama said to the woman. "I'm Claire Cassidy."

Mama put out her hand across the fence. The woman took her hand, then dropped it.

"I'm Phyllis Croft," she said. "We just rented this house for a few months."

"Welcome," said Mama. "We'll have tea sometime."

Mrs. Croft backed up a bit.

"And I have a daughter, Alice, who is probably about Phillip's age. Are you about ten?"

"He's nine," said Mrs. Croft crisply.

She grabbed Phillip's arm and pulled him away.

"We have errands," she said. "Nice to meet you," she added.

"Nice to meet you, Phillip," said Mama. "And you," she quickly added to Mrs. Croft.

Mama and I watched them go back up the steps to their front porch. Phillip turned to look at us. All of a sudden he held his hand up in a small wave.

"Well, Kodi. I'm surprised you *didn't* bite that woman," said Mama.

Kodi wagged his tail.

"I feel sorry for Phillip," I said.

Mama sighed. "I do too."

"Alice is right. He *is* a prisoner," I said. "Mrs. Croft is mean."

Mama seemed thoughtful.

"I wonder . . . ," she began.

I looked up at her, waiting.

"I think she's scared," said Mama.

"Scared of what?"

Mama smiled slightly. "Dogs. She's scared of dogs. And I think . . ." She stopped.

"What?"

"I think maybe she's scared of Phillip."

Mama and I stood at the fence for a moment.

"You cahn't know!" a voice came from inside our house.

"Let's go," said Mama, smiling. "Lena's awake."

As we walked, I turned to look at the Crofts' house and saw Phillip in the window, watching us.

I smiled.

He smiled too.

chapter 3

"He doesn't speak?" asked Alice.

"No," I said.

"No," said Lena.

"Why?" asked Alice.

I shrugged.

"Okay," said Alice. "I can talk."

I smiled.

"You sure can," I said. "You and Lena."

"He doesn't have to talk," said Alice. "That's what Mama said."

But why didn't he talk? Was he afraid? Was he sad? He must have talked once, maybe when he was a baby. When he was little? Maybe he had talked last week.

Why not now?

Daddy finished his coffee.

"I have to go. I have dogs and cats and one donkey to see," he said. "You want me to take Lena to the clinic? She could be a bother here."

"Lena. Bother," said Lena.

Mama smiled. "It's okay. We can put the cover on her cage if she talks too much. That quiets her."

"Funny," I said. "There's a boy next door who doesn't talk and a parrot inside who talks all the time."

"And a man who drives a black car and comes and goes slyly," said Alice.

"Slyly?" I asked.

Alice nodded.

"He's not a king," she said. "He's a spy. Spies don't talk much. They just spy."

Daddy smiled.

"Could be," he said. "Though you seem more like a spy than Mr. Croft."

"I'm a writer," said Alice.

"Kind of like a spy," said Daddy.

Alice smiled as if she knew that.

The phone rang and Mama answered it.

"Hello. . . . Oh yes. . . . Uh-huh. . . . Uh-huh."

"Uh-huh," said Lena, making us laugh.

"I have a leash for her, by the way," said Mama. "See you in the morning, then."

She hung up the phone and leaned down to hug May. Mama's face was very serious.

"May's going to her new home tomorrow?" asked Daddy.

Mama nodded and Daddy put his arm around her.

"I'll miss May," he said.

We'd all miss May. But what Daddy meant was that he knew Mama would miss her most. Mama had rescued May.

"Well, May has a great home in the country," said Mama with a small smile. "With a pond. With a family who will love her. And . . ."

She stopped suddenly.

"And what?" asked Daddy as if he knew what.

"I got a telephone call last night. There are two more dogs coming," said Mama.

Daddy didn't say anything.

"I had to," she said. "They wouldn't be alive in two days, so I'm taking them."

"Two," said Daddy.

"Two. I have to drive across state to pick them up. One is young."

Daddy nodded.

"Two," he said, beginning to laugh.

"Two," said Lena, laughing with Daddy.

The Crofts' house was the only other one we could see from our house. Ours was old. The farmer who owned all the land around it had lived here with its uneven wood floors and lavender wavery glass windows, its five fireplaces and three closets. When the farmer retired, he built the house where the Crofts lived.

The dogs had almost a half acre fenced in for running and digging and sleeping under trees. There were still cattle and horses in the fields surrounding our house. Sometimes Kodi spent time watching over the cows from his side of the fence. It was a Great Pyr's job in life to guard the herd. Kodi kept watch over them in his own way.

The fence was where I found Alice and Phillip, sitting cross-legged with the dogs.

Alice was talking.

"And my father is a vet. He takes care of small and big animals. Mama rescues Great Pyrenees dogs so they won't be killed. We have a talking parrot inside. You can come in to see her if you want."

Kodi and May lay on either side of Phillip, Kodi's big head on his lap.

"Did Mrs. Croft allow Phillip to come inside the fence?" I asked Alice.

"Yes. I told her he was coming over for a visit. I said I'd walk him home when he was ready."

"And?"

"She didn't say anything," said Alice.

I laughed.

A door opened and shut next door. Mrs. Croft stood on the porch.

"Come home soon, Phillip," she called. "We have to go shopping before lunch."

"No, thank you, Mrs. Croft," called Alice.

Mrs. Croft's mouth hung open with surprise.

Alice stood up, and Phillip stood too.

"Phillip's having lunch at our house," she called. "Don't worry. It will be healthy."

Alice took Phillip's hand and they walked toward the house.

"The queen watches," said Alice softly. "Come, royal doggies."

Kodi and May walked on either side of them like guardian angels.

I looked back. Mrs. Croft had gone inside. A little slice of sunlight marked the place she had been.

chapter 4

Inside the kitchen Phillip stared at Lena. Lena slid sideways on her bar perch and bobbed her head, staring back at him.

"Lena's waiting for you to say something," said Alice.

There was a silence.

"Okay," said Alice. "I'll do the talking. Lena, meet Phillip."

"Meet Phillip," said Lena.

Phillip's eyes widened. He grinned and moved his hand for Alice to say something else.

"Phillip is a nice boy, Lena," said Alice.

"Nice boy, Lena," said Lena.

Phillip laughed suddenly. It was the only sound we'd heard from him. It had burst out of him, somehow, like music. It made me think of the cheerful sound of Daddy emptying the coins from his pockets onto the kitchen table.

It made Lena laugh too. Kodi came up and nosed Phillip. Kodi was nearly as tall as Phillip, and somehow Phillip looked small next to Kodi, his skinny arm around Kodi's neck.

"Tomorrow May goes to her new home," said Alice.

Phillip frowned a bit. He reached out and patted May. She sniffed his face, making Phillip close his eyes happily.

Mama put sandwiches on the table.

"Lie down, Kodi. Lie down, May," said Mama. "They can easily reach the table and eat your food," she added.

"Food," said Lena.

Phillip ate quickly. He looked around the sunny kitchen at Lena and the dogs. I wondered what it was like eating with the Crofts next door. Was it quiet? *Too quiet?* One small boy with two grown-ups who didn't seem to know what to do with Phillip?

Of course, Alice the talker said it out loud.

"I bet it is different next door," she said, not expecting Phillip to answer.

He didn't.

"The spy and the queen next door eat at a long, dark table in a long, dark dining room," said Alice, making up a story. "They eat creamed spinach and liver. There is no talk. When there is talk, it is boring.

"'Nice day, dear . . . la-la-la.'

'How do you like my tie? . . .

la-la-la.'

'Lovely liver . . . la-la-la.'

"The boy who lives with them bundles

up the creamed spinach and liver in his napkin and puts it in his pocket. He throws it in the trash when the spy and the queen aren't looking."

Phillip grinned at his toasted cheese sandwich.

But he didn't speak.

chapter 5

"Car," said Alice, peering out the kitchen window.

"Car," said Lena.

Mama stood very still for a moment.

"Okay," she said. "They're early."

May knew the people who were adopting her. She had met them twice—once here, once at their house. I couldn't remember their last name, but their first names were easy. They were both named Tom, man and wife.

"How can that be?" Alice had asked. "Two Toms?"

"He's Tom and she's Tommy," said Mama. "Tomasina, I think."

Alice snorted. And from that time on they were known as the Two Toms.

I watched them get out of the car. The man Tom smiled at the woman Tom, who carried a pot of flowers. They walked up to the porch.

May put her nose in the air and woofed. She was brushed. She was wearing her new green leather collar.

Mama opened the door.

When May saw the Toms, she ran to them and wagged her huge feathered tail.

"May!" the Two Toms said. They often said the same thing at the same time. It seemed to cut down on confusion.

"Don't allow her to jump up on you," warned Mama. "She's too big for that. Say 'off.'"

"Off," said the Two Toms.

"Off!" said Lena loudly.

"Hi, Zoe. Hi, Alice," said the Tom woman.

"Here's her leash," said Mama. She handed them a folder. "And here's the paperwork you'll need for your vet: a list of her vaccinations and early health records. You'll see she's healthy."

The Tom woman leaned over and gave Mama a kiss on the cheek. She handed Mama the flowers. "We thank you. We'll keep in touch, Claire."

"Call me if you have any questions," said Mama. "I'd like to hear how she's doing. She's a good girl."

Surprisingly, it was Alice who had tears. She hugged May, who was loving all this attention even though she didn't understand what was about to happen.

I looked at Kodi, who stood to the side. Tom the man went over and patted Kodi, and Kodi wagged his tail.

But he knew. Kodi always knew that when a new dog came, that dog would go away again.

I moved over and put my hand on his

head. He looked at me with those smart black eyes.

When the Two Toms and May went out the door, Kodi left me and walked to the window and looked out. He watched May stand by the car. We all stood there.

May got into the backseat. She turned her head and looked at us for a moment.

Then she was gone.

It is dark night, only the night-light glowing, when I feel something move next to me in bed. I turn over and see his big face next to my face. He has stretched out on my white down quilt.

White on white.

I smile in the dark and put my arm around his big, soft, furry body.

"It's all right, Kodi," I whisper. "There will be more dogs soon."

Kodi sighs a dog sigh.

He sleeps. All is quiet again.

chapter 6

In the morning Alice, Mama, and Daddy were looking out the kitchen window.

"What's there?" I asked.

"Kodi," Mama said.

Kodi was standing at the fence, looking down the road where May had disappeared.

"He misses May," said Daddy.

"I'll go," Mama said.

But I touched her arm.

"Look," I said.

Phillip walked down the yard toward Kodi. He stopped partway. We could see his lips move. Kodi turned around to look at him, then bounded away from the fence and ran to Phillip. They walked together down to the grove of trees and stopped to look out over the fields of cows.

"He talks," I said. "Phillip said something to Kodi."

"It seems so," said Daddy.

"How come he doesn't talk to the rest of us?" I asked.

"Maybe he doesn't have anything to say to us," said Alice.

"No. Phillip has lots to say," I said. "Lots."

My voice sounded loud in the quiet kitchen.

No one said anything.

"He thinks many things. And those things are trapped inside of him. Maybe something happened that made him afraid to talk," I said.

I looked out the window.

"Except to Kodi," I added softly.

"Kodi and Phillip are friends in some way we don't know about," said Daddy. "And it doesn't have much to do with words."

"Kodi liked Phillip from the very first," said Mama. "You know how Kodi sometimes leaves food for a new dog when we take that dog in, as if he knows the dog needs more? He's that way with Phillip. He's a caretaker."

"You think Phillip needs more? Like a rescue dog?" I asked.

"I do," said Mama. "Don't you?"

Alice sat down at the table and took out her journal.

"Poor Kodi. The dogs come and go and he's always left behind," said Alice.

"Maybe that is what Kodi and Phillip know about each other. They're both left behind," I said.

"Hey, with a very nice family!" said Daddy.

"Don't know that about Phillip's family," said Alice.

Daddy took the cloth cover off Lena's

big cage. "What do you think, Lena?"

"You cahn't know," said Lena.

"What are you writing, Alice?" asked Daddy.

"I'm writing a poem called 'You Cahn't Know,'" said Alice without looking up.

Daddy laughed.

I looked over Alice's shoulder at what she was writing.

"She's telling the truth!" I said, surprised.

"Alice always tells the truth," said Mama, filling Lena's water dish with clean water. "Even if it is fiction."

Day after day Kodi stood at the fence, looking down the road for May. And day after day Phillip came on his own to stand with Kodi, sometimes getting him to play and run.

"Phillip's good with dogs," said Mama. "He should have a dog."

"That won't happen," said Alice.

"I wonder," said Mama.

She took her pineapple angel food cake out of the oven.

"Phyllis Croft is coming over for tea today," she said. "I cornered her this morning."

She put the cake on a plate and took out teacups. She put a bowl of whipped cream on the table for the cake. She put her rose-colored cloth napkins next to the teacups.

"Here?" said Alice. "She's coming here?"

"Here," said Mama. "And you and Zoe can find something else to do."

"She's getting rid of us," I said.

"Do you think that is parental abuse?" asked Alice.

Mama and I laughed.

And then there was a soft knock at the door.

Mama opened the door, and Phyllis Croft and Phillip and Kodi stood there, like three guests come to a party. Mrs. Croft pulled back a bit from Kodi, who seemed to want to lean on her.

"Kodi," warned Mama. "Zoe. You and Alice can have some cake and whipped cream with Phillip out on the porch. Take Kodi with you."

"Bye-bye, Kodi," said Lena.

Mrs. Croft jumped back.

"He talks!" she said, her voice shrill and high.

"He talks," shrieked Lena, imitating Mrs. Croft's voice very well.

"She," said Mama.

"Is she mocking me?" said Mrs. Croft, indignant.

"You cahn't know!" said Lena, as we knew she would.

Surprisingly, Mrs. Croft laughed loudly. It was a little hysterical sounding.

Lena laughed the same way.

"She imitates all of us," said Mama. "It's her way."

Phillip looked shocked that Mrs. Croft had laughed, as if he'd never heard her laugh before.

"All right, children and Kodi. You can take your cake and whipped cream out to the porch," said Mama.

She poured tea in a flowered cup for Mrs. Croft.

We all shuffled out carrying cake, Phillip still staring at Mrs. Croft. After a minute the door opened and Kodi came out too. We sat down at the porch table, Kodi close to Phillip.

We piled whipped cream on our cake.

It was quiet as we ate.

"Yum. I'm not talking," said Alice.

"Me neither," I said.

"And Phillip won't talk," said Alice.

We all grinned big grins, whipped cream oozing over our lips.

"Moo," said Alice like a calf with a mouthful of milk.

We laughed and laughed so much that Kodi woofed at us, and the sun came out from behind a cloud, creeping across the yard and up the steps to warm our feet.

Kodi was in the yard down by the fence watching over the cows in the meadow when Mrs. Croft came out onto the porch.

"Thank you again," she said to Mama in the kitchen. "Come along, Phillip!" she chirped.

"Come along, Phillip," chirped Lena in the kitchen.

Kodi wheeled around when he heard Mrs. Croft's voice. He ran up the yard to the porch.

Phillip waved goodbye and walked down the steps. Kodi nosed Mrs. Croft's hand and, startled, she pulled her hand back. But then she reached out and let Kodi sniff her.

Mrs. Croft looked down at Phillip and said something I couldn't hear. Phillip smiled at her but didn't speak.

Alice was closer to her than I was.

"What did she say to Phillip?" I asked Alice.

Alice smiled. "She said, 'Is that really how I sound?'"

chapter 7

"At least she laughed," said Alice after Phillip and Mrs. Croft had gone home.

"Kind of a laugh," I said. "Sounded like Lena."

Mama dragged a huge dog crate out into the kitchen. She was packing up the car to pick up two new dogs. Some dogs felt better in crates. Some dogs had lived in crates for a long time. Mama always hoped they'd ride free, sitting in the backseat, looking out the windows, leaving nose prints on the glass.

"Mrs. Croft let Kodi sniff her hand when she walked home," I said.

"Really," said Mama with a smile. "That's a good sign."

"Mrs. Croft doesn't seem to understand many things," I said.

"Phyllis doesn't know anything about children, that's for sure," said Mama. "She never had children. Or any dogs or pets. She's had a . . ." Mama searched for words. "She's had an uncluttered life," she said finally. "Except for her husband."

"So why is Phyllis the one to take care of Phillip?" I asked.

Mrs. Croft had become Phyllis to us, even Alice and me, at least in private.

Mama carried two old blankets out to the porch and dumped them.

"She cares about Phillip," said Mama. "In her own way she cares about Phillip. She just doesn't know what to do with him."

"Phillip laughed on the porch," said Alice. "He likes us."

"He laughed," I said. "But he's sad."

Mama looked at me for a moment. Alice was quiet.

"He's sad," I repeated. "And something sad is happening at his home for him to be with Phyllis and Mr. Croft."

Mama put a packet of dog snacks in her pocket.

"You know, under all that fuss that is the outside of Phyllis I think she's nice," said Mama.

"Good thing they moved here," said Alice, writing in her journal.

Mama smiled. "You're right. There's a whole summer for Phillip and Phyllis to work on that."

Mama took the cover off Lena's cage. "Hello, Lena."

"Hello, Lena," said Lena.

"I'll be gone for most of the day, Zoe. You can call Daddy if you need to," said Mama.

"How come I'm not in charge?" asked Alice.

"How come?" repeated Lena, making us laugh.

"You're in charge of you, Alice," said Mama.

"Are you taking Kodi?" I asked.

Sometimes Mama took Kodi when she picked up new dogs. It made the dogs feel more calm to have a peaceful dog in the car with them.

Mama walked to the window and looked out. Phillip had come through the gate and was sitting under a tree with Kodi.

"I think I'll leave Kodi here," Mama said. "They can spend the day together."

Mama packed up the car with water and dog bowls, food, and the crate and blankets.

"Remember," she called to us, "there will be a young dog. Make sure everything is up off the floor!"

Mama got in the car and was gone.

"We haven't had a young dog here in a long time," said Alice. "Remember? Billy was a bad puppy. He ate all my pencils."

"Bad puppy!" said Lena.

Lena liked saying that. She said it more.

"Bad puppy!"

"Bad puppy!"

"Bad puppy!"

chapter 8

It was a warm summer day. Alice and I moved Lena's big cage out under the tree with Phillip and Kodi. There was a breeze, and some of Lena's feathers rippled with the wind.

Lena slid up and down her perch and peered at the cows behind the fence.

There were four of them today, two mothers and their half-grown calves, red brown with white faces. They looked bright and newly washed.

Lena made a sound, like a squawk, a sound she'd never made before.

"She doesn't know what the cows are," said Alice softly. "She has no words for them."

Alice peered at Phillip.

Phillip didn't say anything.

"Cows, Lena. Those are cows," said Alice finally.

Lena was silent.

She squawked again and slid down her perch closer to Phillip.

Phillip stared at her for a moment, then at me.

A breeze came up again.

"Alice, would you go get the cookies in the kitchen? And the glasses? I'll come in a minute and get the lemonade."

"Sure. Be right back," said Alice.

I watched her walk slowly up the hill.

Phillip still looked at me, as if he knew I had something to say.

I leaned over closer to Phillip.

"Lena wants you to talk to her. And you can talk to her in private, just like you talk to Kodi. You don't have to talk to us, Phillip. It's all right."

I got up.

"It means a lot to Kodi," I said.

Kodi lifted his head when he heard his name.

"It means a lot to Lena, too."

Phillip looked at Lena, then back at me.

"I'm going to get the lemonade," I said.

I ran up the hill to catch up with Alice. I tapped her on the arm.

"Don't look back yet," I said to her.

We didn't look back.

"Cows!" said Lena loudly behind us. "Cows!" she said again, sounding happy with herself.

Now Lena had a word for what she saw. And the word from the person she wanted to talk to her.

Alice and I turned and walked backward to the house.

"How did you know?" Alice asked me.

I shrugged my shoulders. "Phillip

knows he doesn't have to talk to us. I knew if he talked to Kodi, he could talk to Lena."

"Funny how Lena wanted Phillip to talk, don't you think?" Alice said.

"Lena likes talk," I said. "It makes her nervous when Phillip is silent."

Behind Phillip and Lena and Kodi the calves butted heads, their mothers patiently moving aside and chewing green grass. We walked up the porch steps.

"Phillip will talk when he has something important to say, I suppose," said Alice as if I had asked her the question.

Which I hadn't.

I had thought about it, though.

❈ ❈ ❈

Daddy came home with pizza for an early dinner. Pepperoni for me. Anchovies for Alice.

"Mama should be home soon," said Daddy. "With your new siblings."

"You really *like* anchovies?" I asked Alice.

"I do. I bet Kodi likes them too. Kodi will eat anything."

"You can't know," said Lena all of a sudden.

"She's talking more like us now," said Alice.

"That happens," said Daddy. "She is living here, so she sounds like us."

It turned out that Kodi didn't like his anchovy. He dropped it on the floor, stared at it, then rolled in it.

"You lost that bet," Daddy said.

Kodi stopped rolling and sat up, listening. He ran to the window.

"Mama," I said.

Kodi wagged his tail. He wagged at Mama getting out of the car with a big dog who looked like him, and a younger spotted dog. They were both on leashes.

We all went out, and Mama let the dogs loose in the yard.

"The big girl is Callie," said Mama. "Jack is the smaller one."

"Quite a big puppy," said Daddy.

"Adolescent," said Mama. "Probably a year old. One day he'll be a big dog like Callie and Kodi."

We knew, from all the dogs who had

come and gone, to be quiet and let the dogs come to us. Kodi went over to Mama to be petted. Callie leaned close to Mama.

"It's okay, Callie," said Mama. Kodi and Callie sniffed each other. Kodi wagged his tail.

Jack rolled over on his back.

"Submissive," said Daddy. "Jack's way of saying 'Yes, you're big and I'm not.'"

Callie came over to Alice to be petted, then me. She looked up into my eyes and sniffed my face. Her nose was soft. I could feel her breath.

I bent down, trying to get Jack to come. It took him a while, but he came to me.

"Jack's the nervous one," said Mama. "He'll need a little work."

Mama looked tired. I knew that rescuing dogs was hard work. She had driven across the state and back to pick up the dogs from another driver, who had picked up the dogs from *another* state. The rescue association didn't always have much money, so drivers from every state volunteered. Callie and Jack had come all the way from Georgia.

Jack, in a sudden burst of energy, jumped up and ran down the yard.

Phillip stood at the fence, watching. He opened the gate and came in, walking down the yard to sit in the grass under the big tree. Kodi went down the yard, Callie following. They ran along the fence together.

Jack walked up and sat in front of Phillip.

Phillip didn't reach out and try to pet Jack. He just sat quietly. After a moment Jack went to sit next to Phillip. Still Phillip didn't touch Jack.

"Look at that," said Mama softly. "What a pair."

Phillip and Jack sat quietly, watching the cows move in the green grass of the meadow, under a blue cloudless sky.

It is dark, with only a slice of moon. Kodi and Callie sleep together on the living-room rug. They don't move when I get a drink of water and pad back to my bedroom. The house is quiet. Alice is sleeping. Mama and Daddy are sleeping. The cover is over Lena's cage. Callie and Jack will meet Lena tomorrow.

When I pull back the covers on my bed, there is Jack, curled up on my sheets with the red poppies on them.

"You," I whisper. Jack lifts his head as if to say, "Yes, it's me."

Then he turns over, and when I lie down next to him, all through the night, I feel the soft rise and fall of his breaths.

chapter 9

"Kodi is happier with new dogs here," I said to Mama in the morning.

Mama nodded. "He's a pack animal. He likes the order of it."

"I guess I'm part of Jack's pack," I said. "He slept with me."

"I saw that when I came in to check

on you in the night," said Daddy. "Jack goes quite well with red poppy sheets."

If Kodi loved having more dogs around, Phyllis next door didn't.

"More dogs?" she said, raising her eyebrows.

She and Mama stood at the fence, on opposite sides.

Daddy came down the yard, his white vet jacket over his shoulder.

"Good morning, Phyllis," he said politely.

Phyllis nodded.

"The dogs need homes," said Mama. Her voice sounded tight to me. It wasn't the way Mama usually sounded. "It's what I've chosen to do. I save them. I take care of them. I know you understand.

You do the very same thing with Phillip, you know."

Phyllis took a little step backward. She was very quiet.

Alice and I were pretending not to listen. But there was no more to hear. Mama moved away, leaving Phyllis looking after her.

"Claire works hard at it," said Daddy.

He put on his jacket. It said DR. CASSIDY on the pocket.

"As do you, Phyllis," said Daddy.

He walked down the yard to say goodbye to Mama, leaving Phyllis just like Mama had.

After a moment Phyllis turned and walked back through the grass, and over the narrow place in the brook, to her house. She walked up the porch steps, standing there to look back at all of us.

"Poor Phyllis," I said in a soft voice.

"What do you mean?" asked Alice.

"I don't know. Poor Phyllis doesn't understand much of our world."

Alice nodded.

"Almost as if she missed too many days of school," said Alice.

I smiled.

"That's a nice way to say it," I said.

"I'm a writer," said Alice. "I put words to things. But you *know* all those things, Zoe."

I stared at Alice, surprised.

In the yard the dogs, all of them, tumbled and ran and played as if they understood all there was to know.

And maybe they did.

It was the next day that life changed for all of us.

It was the day that it happened.

It would be a rainy day.

The cows would graze in the meadow.

Far off the horses would run when the wind came up.

But the next day would be the day that it happened.

chapter 10

It was dark when I heard the phone ring. Then there were voices. Loud voices. I looked at my clock. It was ten. Next to me Callie slept.

Callie? Where was Jack?

When I got out of bed, I saw that the outside house lights were on, even the spotlights that lit up the fenced-in yard.

Kodi was staring out the windows of the kitchen. He ran to the door asking to go out.

Daddy came in the door, wearing a wet slicker.

"What's the matter?" I asked.

I rubbed my eyes.

"Jack got out," said Daddy. "Mama's going after him."

"How?"

"The gate was open. He ran off."

Daddy grabbed a plastic bag of dog snacks and the big flashlight.

"Are you going too?" I asked.

Daddy shook his head. "I have an emergency. Mama will have to handle it. She'll be all right. She's been through this before."

Mama came into the kitchen, and I could hear heavy rain in the darkness outside.

"I'm going to take Kodi," she said. "He'll help find Jack. Zoe, you'll have to keep Callie calm. She might be scared that the other dogs are gone."

"She's sleeping on my bed," I said.

"Well, good. Give her snacks, play with her. Anything to keep her happy."

Mama slipped the leash over Kodi's head. He wagged his tail and pranced, ready to go out.

"Don't worry, Zoe. We'll be back sometime. And I have my cell phone, if it works in this weather."

Mama and Kodi were gone.

I looked through the window and saw wind and rain in the lit backyard.

"I'll be at the clinic, but you can call if you need me," said Daddy.

And then Daddy was gone too.

It was quiet in the kitchen. Alice was sleeping. Callie was sleeping.

I sat at the kitchen table.

I thought about Jack out in the rain and dark.

At least Mama and Kodi had each other while they searched.

But Jack was alone.

A clap of thunder made me jump. I heard Callie whimper in my bedroom.

I went in and lay down next to her. I put my arm around her and felt her shaking.

"It's all right, Callie," I whispered. "The thunder will be gone soon. The rain will be gone soon. Everything will be all right."

She stopped shaking. She slept.

I slept some, but the rain and wind kept waking me.

But in the morning, at first light, the rain had not gone.

And everything was not all right.

chapter 11

I woke hearing rain. And pounding at the kitchen door.

I got up and saw Phyllis Croft at the door. She wore a raincoat, but her hair was wild and wet. She looked like a child.

I opened the door and she rushed in.

"Is Phillip here?" she demanded. "Where are your mother and father?"

I took her coat and shook the rain off of it. I hung it on a hook by the door.

"Jack got out last night. He ran off, and my mother went after him," I said. "Daddy had an emergency."

"Where's Phillip?" she said.

Alice came into the kitchen in her pajamas.

"What's happening?" she asked.

"I can't find Phillip," said Mrs. Croft.

She sat in a kitchen chair and began to cry.

"His bed hasn't been slept in," she said.

Tears came down her face.

"It's my fault," she said. "His parents

called and he heard me talking to them. They've been having trouble. I screamed at Phillip to talk to me! I needed to know what he was thinking! And now he's gone."

Alice looked quickly at me.

"We were the only relatives able to take him," said Phyllis. "I don't know anything about children. I don't know anything about Phillip!"

"They've been having trouble?" I repeated. It was half a question, half me talking to me. Telling myself something.

"Does Phillip know about their trouble?" I asked.

"I think so," she said. "But he doesn't speak!"

"Did he see the lights on last night?"

I asked. "The lights in the yard?"

Mrs. Croft nodded. "We all saw them. But where would he go in the pouring rain? Maybe he wanted to get away from me! It's my fault. I shouldn't have screamed at him."

Alice sat next to Mrs. Croft and took her hand.

"It's not your fault," she said. "It's no one's fault."

Suddenly, I knew why Phillip wouldn't talk. Couldn't talk. And I knew where Phillip had gone.

I ran to my bedroom and pulled on my jeans and sweater. Callie turned over and looked at me from the bed.

I ran back into the kitchen and pulled on my boots.

"Phillip went to save Jack," I said.

"Out in this rain? For a dog?" said Mrs. Croft.

"For a dog who loves Phillip," I said.

I put dog snacks into a plastic bag. I picked up a rolled-up dog blanket.

"Alice, get me two bottles of water. Daddy will be home soon from the clinic. Mama will call on her cell phone."

"What? What are you doing?" asked Mrs. Croft.

I put on my slicker.

"Alice, take care of Callie. She doesn't like the rain. She might miss me. She might miss the dogs."

I stopped then.

"Are you all right alone?" I asked Alice.

Alice nodded.

"I'll stay with her," said Mrs. Croft. She started to cry again.

"We'll stay with each other," said Alice.

I put some breakfast biscuits in my pockets, and some lumps of sugar.

We could hear the sound of pellets hitting the windows. *Hail*.

"I'm going to find Phillip," I said.

I opened the door and went out of the warm kitchen into the cold.

I put up my slicker hood and hurried down to the meadow. The rain and hail pellets sounded loud against my slicker. My pant legs were already wet. The rain came down harder, and there was thunder.

I passed the cows, who stood under the big tree in the meadow. They stood in a comforting group, like a cow family.

I thought of Jack, lost in a place he didn't know. I thought of Phillip, who couldn't call for help. Phillip, who wouldn't talk because he thought his mother and father's problems might be his fault—something he'd said, perhaps. His silence might keep them all safer.

And, like Phyllis, I began to cry.

chapter 12

I hurried down to the meadow. My wet pant legs were cold.

I ran to the nearest barn to get out of the rain. Mama had been out all night looking for Jack. She hadn't called because she knew Alice and I were sleeping. She had Kodi. Jack had no one. Phillip had no one.

Inside the barn the horses in their stalls peered at me.

"Phillip? Jack?" I called. "It's Zoe."

I knew Mama and Kodi had been here. They would have come here first.

There was silence except for the snorting of horses.

I put my hood back up and ran outside again, across the dirt road, to the next meadow.

The sky grew even darker and the rain came harder.

I ducked between the rails of the gate and ran through the mud to a yellow barn.

It was suddenly quiet in the barn, and strangely peaceful. The horses rolled their eyes at me.

Who are you?
Do you have a carrot?
A lump of sugar?

I did have some lumps of sugar that I'd stashed in my pockets along with some breakfast biscuits, dog treats, and two bottles of water. I couldn't remember why I had put the sugar in my pockets, but now I was glad.

The horses were glad too. The four of them crowded around, and I fed them all sugar lumps.

"Phillip? Phillip, are you here?" I called. "Jack! Mama!?"

No answer from Mama.

Of course Phillip wouldn't answer. I would have to search every stall.

The horses had stepped back when

I raised my voice. I went from stall to stall, looking in each one for a dog or two and a boy.

In one stall was a pile of hay. There was a small scooped-out place where someone or something had rested. I leaned down and saw it—a clump of dog hair. I picked it up. It wasn't Kodi's pure white hair that I knew so well. It was mottled, black and white.

Jack's hair.

But where were they? And where was Mama?

Suddenly, I heard a new sound. It was bigger hail hitting the barn roof. It started light at first, then grew heavier.

The horses were restless with the new sound. I looked out the door and saw hail hitting the ground, collecting in places like little bits of glass. The sky was even darker now.

I had to go now before the hail got larger and the wind grew stronger. I put my hood up and ran across the paddock and across the road, looking for another hiding place. I thought Phillip would hide from this weather. I didn't know about Jack. He might still be running somewhere. I ducked in a lean-to shed filled with garden tools and a lawn mower.

But then, Phillip might still be running after Jack too.

Mama wouldn't take Kodi out in hail. Rain maybe, but not hail.

I ran across a meadow until I got to

a large tree. I joined more cows there. The tree was large enough to keep us all safe from hail. The cows looked at me, then went back to eating grass.

I could see a hay barn across the paddock, a barn I'd never seen before. The door was open. As the hail came down faster and harder, I ran across the mud to the open door and went inside.

It was a barn with only a few windows, and I could smell the sweet smell of the bales of hay stored there for the cows and horses.

I walked in the path between the neat bales that were bound with twine. The farmer was neat too. The old wood floors were smooth and clean, as if the farmer had swept them.

White Fur Flying

I walked on without calling out. The hail had grown heavier or bigger, I couldn't tell. But the noise filled the barn.

And then, when I passed the last neat bales, in the very back of the barn, when I was about to give up, I found them.

Phillip and Jack.

Phillip was asleep in a loose pile of hay, Jack sleeping next to him, curled close to Phillip. I didn't say anything. I sat down next to Jack. He raised his head and looked at me the way he had when he slept on my red poppy sheets, and then put his head back down in the hay and went back to sleep. I stroked his body and he didn't move. He was warm.

My throat felt tight. I could feel tears at the edges of my eyes. Suddenly, I felt so tired. The noise of hail and wind was steady, and Jack and Phillip slept on.

I pulled my rain jacket around me and lay back in the hay. I turned on my side so I could see them. I watched them for a long time.

And then I slept.

chapter 13

It was the quiet that woke me. There were no sounds of wind and rain and hail. I opencd my eyes, and light was coming in one of the windows.

Phillip and Jack were sitting up in the hay, looking at me.

"Jack saved me," said Phillip right away.

"He ran ahead of me, but when I got lost, he came back and led me to a barn. But when we were hidden in the hay, the farmer came in, so we ran out. We ran and ran. It started to hail and we found this place. We were both very tired."

I sat up.

"Are you all right, Zoe?" he asked suddenly.

I didn't say "Phillip, you're talking!" because I didn't want him to stop and I was afraid he'd be shy and silent again.

I smiled at him.

"I know," he said, as if he'd read my thoughts. "I'm talking. I know."

He stroked Jack, who leaned into him and fell over in a heap so Phillip could rub his stomach.

"I'm glad," I said. "And I'm glad you're safe. Both of you. I looked everywhere."

"I knew you would," he said. "And I knew your mama would."

"And I did," said Mama, standing in front of us with Kodi. Kodi's tail wagged when he saw Phillip.

"Mama!"

I jumped up and put my arms around her. She was wet. Her hair was plastered down around her face. Kodi was wet too.

"I knew," said Phillip.

Mama hugged Phillip. She didn't say anything about his talking either.

"Let's go," said Mama.

She put the leash on Jack, and we followed her outside. It was clearing now, and the air was fresh and sharp. Everything looked new.

Mama dialed her phone. She waited a moment.

"Hello," she said. "We're on our way." She listened.

"Yes. All of us," she said.

She snapped her cell phone shut and smiled at us. "Let's go home."

chapter 14

We walked back home together, three people and two dogs, one person talking all the way.

"Jack was a hero," said Phillip. "A true hero. He found me and led me where it was safe."

I took off my rain slicker and put it around Mama.

"And he was never scared or scatty. 'Scatty' is what my aunt Phyllis says sometimes. That's funny, don't you think?" said Phillip. "Coming from her?"

Mama smiled.

"Yes," she said.

"Phyllis isn't so scatty today," I said. "She is sitting in our house with Alice and Callie. She's probably crying."

"Crying?" asked Phillip. "Why?"

"She thought it was her fault you were lost," I said. "She had screamed at you. She wanted you to talk."

"And now I do," said Phillip.

No one said anything. We crossed

meadows and fields. We crossed two dirt roads I didn't remember crossing.

The cows looked like they'd had baths, all clean and shiny. The horses ran by the fences when we passed.

"Hello, horses," said Phillip. "Hello, cows. Remember those horses, Jack? We were in the barn with them. We made a little nest in the hay."

"I found that nest," I said. "I found a bit of Jack's hair."

I put my hand in my pocket and gave the clump to Phillip.

"There it is," I said.

Phillip smelled it.

"That's Jack's hair," he said, and we laughed.

We walked by the barn at the end of

our meadow. The cows looked up and went back to eating.

We walked up past the fence to our yard. Callie came running and leaping with excitement. Alice smiled at us and waved. Phyllis stood next to her. Daddy was on the porch standing next to a policeman. A police car stood at the curb, its whirling lights still on.

Mr. Croft's black car drove into his driveway. He got out and walked down the yard.

He opened his mouth to speak. We had never heard him speak up to now, but Mama spoke before he could.

"Phyllis, thank you for being so patient. As it turned out, Zoe found Phillip and Jack, but I should tell you—"

Mr. Croft started to say something.

"Wait."

It was Phillip interrupting both Mama and Mr. Croft this time.

"Let me tell it," said Phillip.

Mr. Croft stopped trying to talk.

"Jack is this brave dog who saved me in the storm. He led me into one barn, then into another safe place when it started to hail and was so windy. . . ."

Everyone stared. Alice smiled.

And as Phillip went on to tell the story, I didn't hear him anymore. All I saw was Phyllis kneel down to put her arms around Phillip. It didn't stop Phillip from talking.

"I was foolish to run after Jack, I suppose, but I love Jack. And then we slept in the hay until Zoe came and her mama and Kodi, and then . . ."

Phyllis, not crying anymore, sat down in the wet grass and put her arms around Jack, who seemed to like it very much. Then she hugged Kodi, who, of course, wagged his tail. And when Phyllis pulled away, there was wet white fur all over her navy blue sweater and slacks.

In the end Mr. Croft never did speak, almost as if he'd taken over Phillip's role as the silent one. And when Mr. Croft and Phyllis and Phillip went across the grass and over the brook and up the steps to their house, Jack followed them.

"Jack!" called Mama.

Phyllis turned around.

"Oh, Claire, please let him come. We'll take care of him. Don't worry."

And she opened the door and they went inside.

chapter 15

It was quiet. Kodi and Callie slept in a heap on the rug. Even Lena was quiet for the time being, as if she knew that it was quiet we all needed.

Daddy put his arms around Mama for a long time.

"Do you want something to eat?" he asked her.

Mama shook her head. "I'm too tired to eat."

There was a small silence.

"I was scared," said Alice finally. "Phyllis was scared too."

Mama smiled.

"Yes," she said. "I didn't know that Zoe was out in the terrible weather. But I was scared for Phillip and Jack."

Mama paused.

"But both Phillip *and* Jack turned out to be different than I thought they were," she added. "There are some things you can't know."

Alice looked up.

"Zoe?" asked Daddy.

"I'm not sure what happened," I said. "I fell asleep in the hay, and when I woke up, Phillip was talking."

"And probably still is," said Daddy with a smile.

"I think Phillip's silence was for protection," I said. "If he said nothing, he couldn't be responsible for his mother and father's troubles."

"That's what Phyllis said," said Alice.

"Everything changed," I said. "It was like something magical happened."

"For a while that something magical was Kodi," said Daddy. "But then that something magical was . . ."

"Jack," I said.

"Yes," said Mama. "It was Jack at the end."

"And now Phyllis is over in her house with white fur flying around the room, attaching itself to the sapphire blue drapes and couches and on her navy blue sweater and slacks and Mr. Croft," said Alice.

She wrote something down in her journal and sat back.

"I'm done," she said. She put down her pen.

"Done," said Lena suddenly.

"With what?" asked Daddy.

Alice opened the rings of her notebook and handed a page to Daddy.

He read it:

"You Can't Know
You can't know that I have everything to say
Even if I don't speak.
You can't know that I have nothing to say
Even if I speak always.

You can't know what I know in my dog mind
Because I have no words.
You can't know, ever, but you should,
That a dog will save you."

When Daddy finished, it was quiet. Except for Lena. And when she spoke, it was almost a whisper.

"You can't know."

chapter 16

Sometimes you think you know more than you really do—people, events, things that are true and things that are not. Sometimes you think you know yourself. But then, surprise, it is someone else who shows you what is really there, like the truth a photograph shows.

It was Alice's journal that turned a light on the day that Phillip was lost and began to speak. Alice is, after all, what Daddy calls the real spy.

It was soon after all that had happened—on a summer day, no wind—when Alice showed it to us.

ALICE'S JOURNAL

Our life is back to the same. Maybe a little bit the same.

Of all of us Zoe is the hero. She's quiet and doesn't say as much as I do, but she's the hero. She went out in the rain and hail and wind all by herself that day to find Phillip and Jack. I should try to be more like Zoe.

Phyllis and I had a long time to talk. Mama was right. Underneath everything I thought she was, Phyllis is nice.

When I asked her if Mr. Croft was a spy, she laughed for a long time. She laughed a nice laugh, not a Lena laugh. I'm not disappointed to find out that Mr. Croft is a librarian! Think of a life surrounded by books and quiet.

I told Phyllis that was more exciting than a spy. I asked her if he talked, and she told me he was more comfortable with books than with people.

"Does he know books and people are the same thing?" I asked.

Phyllis smiled at me

"Not always," she said.

Phillip adopted Jack as his own rescue dog. They are happy. He has gone home to his parents, who solved their problem. Phillip hasn't stopped talking. He writes us very talky letters.

We have adopted Callie. She and Kodi are soul mates, Daddy says.

Phyllis and the silent Mr. Croft decided to stay in the rental house next door for a year. Phyllis is very fond of Callie and Kodi. They visit her often, brushing up against her drapes and lying on her furniture. Phyllis is getting quite good at cleaning white fur flying off her furniture and clothes and Mr. Croft.

Sometimes when Mr. Croft goes out to his car in his dark suit,

Phyllis comes running after him, rolling
a sticky tape up and down his
trousers.

Daddy has not found a home
for Lena. It may be a secret to
everyone, even to Daddy, but I
think he loves Lena. I have started
reading poetry to her, and Lena
spouts it back.

"I wandered lonely as a cloud!"

"How do I love thee? Let me
count the ways."

"Shall I compare thee to a
summer's day?"

And Lena's favorite, a Mary Oliver
poem:

I have a little dog who likes to nap
with me.

He climbs on my body and puts his
face in my neck
He is sweeter than soap.

Lena's version, while short, is still
poetry. She says, "I have a little
dog . . . sweeter than soap."
Then we put the cover over her
cage.
Mama has new dogs coming. It
is no secret to anyone that Mama
loves to rescue dogs.
Things change.
Things don't change.
Lena's right.
You can't know.

—Alice Cassidy

Author's Note

Thousands of Pyrs and Pyr mixes, as well as other abandoned dogs, end up in shelters across the country. It takes a great deal of work to find homes for them, but the good news is that there are many people rescuing, fostering, and adopting these dogs. My daughter,

Emily, and her family have adopted a Great Pyr mix, and he is a gentle, sweet, big dog. I have written about him in my book *Waiting for the Magic*. His name is Neo.

Dogs make great friends and companions to all ages of people.

If you go to NationalPyr.org you can see the many Great Pyr dogs waiting for adoption, and those who have found homes.

Patricia MacLachlan

Everyone in Lucy's family sings.

Everyone, except Lucy.

Lucy can't sing;

her voice won't come out.

JUST LIKE SINGING, helping Aunt Frankie
prepare for flooding season is a family
tradition—even if Frankie doesn't want it.
But when the flood arrives, Lucy will need to
find her voice to save her little brother.

Secrets

We drive across the Minnesota prairie in our old tan and green Volkswagen bus. My father does not believe in new cars. He loves the old Volkswagen with the top that pops up like a tent. He can take the motor apart and fix it himself.

In the way back are neat wooden

framed beds for sleeping. In a pen are Mama's chickens: Ella, Sofia, and Nickel. Mama loves them and never goes away for long without them. My younger sister, Grace, sits in her car seat next to me. In back of her is Teddy, the youngest, with his stuffed beaver.

My father, called Boots because he wears them, is driving, listening to opera on the radio. It is *La Traviata.*

Misterioso, misterioso altero . . .

I know it well. If a conductor dropped dead on stage I could climb up there and conduct.

Now here is something abnormal. I can't sing. When I open my mouth nothing happens. I know the music, but I can't sing it. I can only conduct it.

My father went to Harvard. His parents expected him to be a banker like his father. In secret he planned to be a poet.

But then he discovered cows. He became a farmer.

He loves cows.

"They are poetry, Lucy," he tells me. "I can't write anything better than a cow."

Maggie, my mother in the front seat, wears headphones. I know she is listening to Langhorne Slim. She loves Langhorne Slim as much as my father loves opera. And I know *her* secret. She would like to sing like Langhorne Slim. She would like to *be* Langhorne Slim.

If you've got worries, then you're like me.
Don't worry now, I won't hurt you.

My younger sister, Gracie, ignores the opera and my mother's bopping around in the front seat. Gracie sings in a high perfect voice, fluttering her hands like birds.

"The birdies fly away, and they come
back home.
The birdies fly away, and they come
back home."

I turn and look at my little brother, Teddy. He smiles at me and I know what that smile is all about.

In his small head he is singing the "Fly Away" chorus in private so no one can hear.

Fly away, fly away,
All the birdies fly away.

I smile back at him.

This is our secret because Teddy wants it that way.

I have known for a long time that Teddy can sing perfectly in tune even though he is not yet two. We all know he doesn't speak words yet. But only Teddy and I know that he sings. He doesn't sing the words, but sings every song with *"la la la."* He sings to me every night, climbing out of his bed, padding into my room in the dark. He sings a peppy "Baa, Baa, Black Sheep," ending with a "Yay" at the end with his hands in the air.

"La La La La
LaLaLaLaLa.
Yay!"

He sings a soft, quiet "All the Pretty Horses." *"La, la, la."*

I made a mistake once and told them all—Boots, Mama, and Gracie—that Teddy can sing. They didn't believe me. And of course Teddy wouldn't sing for them. Only for me.

"I've never heard Teddy sing," says Gracie.

"He can't even talk yet," says Mama. "How could he sing?"

Teddy has music but no words.

I have words but no music.

We are a strange pair.

And here is *my* secret: I am planning to be a poet. I have written thirty-one and a half poems. Some are bad. They are bad hideaway poems. I plan to get better and publish better poems and buy Mama more chickens and take Boots to see *La Traviata* at the opera house in New York City, wherever New York City is.

When I get to be a poet Boots will be pleased.

He will be proud.

And one day, for him, I will write a poem as beautiful as a cow.

Cow

The reason we have all been loaded into the old bus is that we spend part of every summer with Aunt Frankie in North Dakota. Everyone calls her Frankie. Her name is Francesca, but she says that is pretentious. That is the first time I ever heard the word "pretentious," and I've been looking for a time to use it ever since. It is much too long for a poem.

Frankie, who Mama says is as "old as time," lives far out in the middle of the universe. She lives by a big river that floods in the rainy season. It is now the rainy season, and Boots says it will flood while we're there.

"Frankie will need our help even though she doesn't think so," says Boots.

"She is so stubborn," my mother complains.

Boots looks at me in the rearview mirror. It is like looking into my eyes, we look so much the same.

He smiles.

"Who else is stubborn?" he asks.

"Mama!" says Gracie.

Frankie has a few milking cows she milks every day, but leases most of the higher meadowland for other people's cattle.

There are few trees, no mountains, just miles and miles of prairie grass and gophers and sky.

And the river.

Frankie's house is the house where Mama grew up. Mama loved it and hated it at the same time. She always cries when we get there and cries when we leave. Maybe one day I'll understand that.

"It sounds like 'the birdies fly away and come back home' to me," I once said to Boots.

"You're very right," he said, peering at me as if I'd said something important.

At dusk we find a place to stop for the night. It is a state park hill with an open field, bordered by a farmland fence. Mama lets Sofia, Ella, and Nickel out of their crates and spreads chicken feed on the ground for them. They flap their wings and mosey around, eating and strutting. My mother and father get out their chairs and their small stove. They set up their tent near a tree. Gracie, Teddy, and I always sleep in the car beds, Teddy in the middle. Mama and Boots could sleep in the bus, but they love their small domed tent.

"Why can't we stay in a motel?" Gracie asks. "Trini's family goes to a motel with a pool and dining room and miniature golf course where a little volcano goes off if you get a hole in one."

I know what Boots is about to say. I've heard it many times. I've even written a poem about it. Gracie has heard it before too, but she is young enough to think the answer may change when she asks to stay in a motel. She'll know better one day.

Motel Room

Where's the river?
Where's the sky?
Can't see the clouds—
Or bluebirds fly by.

Boots waves his arm.

"In a motel you wouldn't have this great view," says Boots. "You'd have four walls with boring paintings."

"Maybe a motel would have a pool," said Gracie.

"Maybe we'll find a river," said Boots.

Can't smell the flowers,
Can't smell the sea—
Four walls and bad art
Is all that you'll see.

I take Teddy for a walk in the meadow. He reaches up and takes my hand with his tiny hand. His hand is warm. He wears red sneakers and a faded T-shirt with a green fish on it.

Suddenly Teddy stops. He is staring at something. He points.

"Cow," he says.

"Teddy, you said cow!"

As far as I know Teddy has never said cow. But he says it as clear as light. He says it again.

"Cow."

"Mama!" I shout. "Boots! Teddy said cow!"

Mama waves. Boots and Gracie come quickly across the field and look where Teddy is pointing. Far off, at the fence, stands a cow. It is a kind of cow I've never seen. Ever.

"Oh, my." Boots's voice is strange. "Oh, my," he repeats.

"Cow," says Teddy again.

"Oh, my," says Boots again.

I feel like I'm in a strange echo chamber.

Boots starts to walk toward the fence, then comes back to scoop Teddy up in his arms. He beckons for us to follow.

At the fence is a very large cow. She is beautiful and black, with a wide white stripe around the middle of her. My breath catches. Maybe Boots is right after all. That he couldn't write anything more beautiful than a cow. Maybe no one can.

"Cow," says Teddy.

"I know that," I say, then I laugh because it is Teddy I'm answering.

"Dutch Belted," says Gracie. "Boots's cows are mostly Holsteins or Guernseys," she tells me.

Gracie has a chart at home of all the cow breeds. She opens her notebook and takes out a pen. She begins to draw the cow.

"I've never seen one," says Boots. He puts his hand across the fence and the cow moves back quickly. Then, after a moment, she comes back so Boots can rub her head.

"Beautiful," says Boots. "Beautiful Dutch Belted."

"Cow," says Teddy.

"Yes, Teddy," says Boots. "Dutch Belted."

Teddy reaches his hand over the fence and rubs the cow's head, imitating Boots. The cow's tongue comes out, long and rough, making Teddy jump.

The sun goes down behind the far-away line of trees. Two more Dutch

Belted cows move toward us, probably hoping for grain.

"Cow," whispers Teddy, putting his arm around Boots's neck.

Nighttime. Grace is sleeping. She is always first to go to sleep. There are stars out in the black sky and I can see the glow of the lantern light in Mama and Boots's tent. There is a slice of moon above the trees.

"See?"

It is Teddy's little voice next to me. That's the only part of my name, Lucy, that he can say— the "see" of Lucy.

"Teddy," I whisper.

"Cow," he says.

"Cow," I whisper.

His eyes gleam in the dark. I know he's

going to sing now. *And he does. He sings the song perfectly, all the la la's in tune. I hear the words in my head.*

> *"Fly away, fly away,*
> *All the birdies fly away."*

I reach over and take his hand.
And we sleep.